Numb

Numb, Volume 2

Raymond Moore

Published by Raymond Moore, 2024.

NUMB

First edition. February 19, 2024.

Copyright © 2024 Raymond Moore.

ISBN: 979-8224283712

Written by Raymond Moore.

For all the bad guys in Glasgow

My name is Coulter Caine, and my game is to take down bad guys in Glasgow. I was born with a rare medical condition called Chronic Insensitivity to Pain and Anhydrosis, or CIPA for short. This means that I don't feel physical pain. After my parents were murdered by the infamous Ballater Boy's, I decided it was time for Glasgow to have its own superhero.

I may not have any superpowers, but I hold a 9th degree Red Belt in Gracie Jiu-Jitsu and I've a passion for technology. Also, let's just say I have a fuckton of money at my disposal. After offing one of the three Ballater brothers and his crew, I've made it my mission to protect the most vulnerable of our dear green place. I want the streets to be safer for you and yours. If I had a mission statement, it'd probably be something like: 'Kicking bad guys cunts in.' If I had a business card that's what I'd put on it! All joking aside though. Let me make one the crystal fucking clear – if you do wrong in our city. If you prey on the weak, the elderly or those who can't defend themselves – you fucking better watch out because Numb's about.

After my bilateral arm surgery, Dr. Assiri and Dr. Manfred finally allowed me to return to the gym to start rebuilding my upper body strength. As a surprise gesture Dr Assiri, who had gotten to know me and my plans for Numb, gave me a special gift as a thank you for letting him use me as a test subject for his endoskeleton. Honestly, I should've been the one thanking him, but it was a kind gesture and it would definitely help me and my crime-fighting pursuits. Bless his Saudi Arabian heart, he gifted me with three Second-Skin-Suits. You're probably wondering what the fuck those are; well, allow me to explain. These suits were originally designed for patients with third-degree burns all over their bodies. The elasto-polymer material applies constant pressure limiting the growth of scar tissue. Dr. Assiri's company took this idea and developed a new molecule for the material that not only applied pressure but also acted as a flexible exoskeleton to protect against bone damage. They kind of looked like those full-body swimsuits you see at the Olympics. Wearing one under my tracksuit provided and extra layer of protection for my recovering bones. Fucking yaas man! I have to admit, when I first put on the suit, I felt like a bit of a fanny. But after wearing it for a few hours around Base, I got used to it. Dr. Manfred suggested that I wear the Second-Skin-Suit all the time. With Dr. Assiri on my team he became one of five. Five people who knew all about Numb and my plans to kick bad guy arse.

During my downtime, I kept a beady eye on the activities of the remaining Ballater brothers. It was no surprise that after the untimely and quite frankly grisly demise of their brother, the bawbags had stepped up their personal security measures. Whenever they travelled from their luxurious homes in Kirkie to their offices in the Saltmarket, it was like a fucking presidential convoy. A black Range Rover lead the way for their company Jags, and a black Transit van followed behind – similar to the one Benny used to drive before he took the final bath of his life. The increased security didn't bother me; it just meant I'd have to be more creative when the time came to fuck them for good. But there was no need to rush; those cunts could wait until I was completely ready.

Jasmine was worried. You know. Concerned about our security. What with my black eyes and broken arms and that. The reality of what I'd begun had really hit home – she knew there was no stopping me though. We agreed that she should move in with me, just in case. She already spent most of her time at mine so it made sense. She'd still keep her flat in Byres Road. Jas had some brilliant ideas for improving our home security, which I began implementing during my arm rehabilitation. First on the list was upgrading all of the security cameras at Base and our house, each equipped with their own solar-charged battery to prevent any cunt from cutting of the power and leaving us vulnerable to attack. We also installed military-grade motion sensors throughout the properties, inside and out. Micro-CCTV cameras were installed at both ends of our street, including the Great Western Road access. To further secure the gaff, we now had blast-proof automatic shutters on every window and door. Iron curtains we call them in Glasgow – hidden from sight until a full lockdown was initiated. Access to all the security measures was controlled from our phones and our bio-metric data on touch panels throughout Base and the house. Khaled had installed an electromagnetic pulse generator in all rooms with computer hard drives. My phone had the self-destruct app that would set of an EMP and completely fry everything containing sensitive information. Really fucking hope I don't have to use it but it was nice to have the option. Most of my sensitive shit was secured in the cloud. I had a server in fucking Switzerland of all places. It was Khaled that sorted it all out. He said the Swiss were good with money and excellent at keeping secrets.

A few weeks ago, I met up with big Gerry over coffee in Springburn. My main goal was to discuss his willingness to assist me with my plans for the upcoming year. I made it clear that I'd totally understand if it was too fucking dangerous for him. I didn't want to put him or his family at risk. Cunt laughed as he reminded me he didn't have a family anymore, not in Glasgow anyway. His wife left him about a year after their son died, and his daughter lived in Aberdeen. The big man was on his tod with only his vast collection of country and western records for company. Thank fuck he was more than a little eager to help me take down anyone causing trouble in the city. To sweeten the deal, I increased his monthly retainer, but I had a feeling that he would help me for free if I asked him. The big man loved being an Uber driver. He said it gave him the time to pursue his hobbies whatever the fuck that meant, though he did admit that it could be a bit fucking boring driving cunts about Glasgow. Helping me added a wee bit of spice to his life, so he said. As we discussed further, Gerry came up with a brilliant idea: I should have a couple of 'safe houses' scattered throughout the city just in case Base got compromised. Have to give it to the big man. I hadn't even thought of it. It was a fucking excellent idea. He even suggested buying a place in Springburn, but I had other plans.

As soon as I got home, I talked it over with Jas. She fucking loved it especially once we started looking at apartments down by the river. My failed attempt at using Packie as a kite had a positive outcome – near his old building was the Lancefield Quay development. A quick call to an estate agent provided info on a top floor apartment with four bedrooms. New to the market. The price was surprisingly reasonable, but there was a catch: the building issue with its cladding. A fucking fire hazard or something. The estate agent said the developer is fixing the problem but that's why the price was pretty good. I made a cash offer on the phone, ten percent below the asking price, and it was accepted. We'd be getting the keys in a week! In addition, I also put in an offer for a wee one-bedroom place in a tenement in Govan Hill. It was located near Cathcart Road, making it the perfect little bolt hole. Khaled would set up a mini-Base in both of them once all the paperwork and shit was done.

There's one more thing I want to mention: I received a letter. An actual fucking letter, I mean, who sends letters these days? This particular one had a Monaco stamp on it and it was from a private bank informing me that my dad's account had been successfully transferred over to my name. Honestly, I hadn't a fucking scooby about what they were on about. What fucking account? I even pulled out the will, but there was no mention of a bank account in Monaco. I immediately called our lawyer, the one who handled mum and dads estate. They told me that there was a letter from dad in their safe, with instructions for me to read once the Monaco account was officially mine. Without wasting any time, I jumped the Subway to Buchanan Street and walked to the lawyers George Square office. John Lansbury, one of the partners, greeted me and invited into his office for a cup of tea.

"What's this all about, John?" I asked. "Why have I never heard about this Monaco account before?"

"Your father wanted it kept confidential, Coulter," replied John. "We don't know why exactly, but his instructions were quite specific with regards to the letter we are holding for you. Once the account transfer was complete we were to give you his letter. He wanted everything to remain hush hush. We knew nothing about the bank account until he came to us a week before... You know... A week before the accident."

John handed me an envelope with dads handwriting on it.

"This is bizarre. My dad keeping secrets. Why am I only finding out about this account now?"

"Monaco banking laws, they do things at their own pace there," smiled John. "Especially with the type of account your dad had."

"So in here are official bank papers?" I asked.

"No Coulter, it's a personal letter from your dad. All of the account documents are with us."

The handwritten letter from dad caught me of guard. Left me feeling winded, if you want to know the honest truth.

"Do I have to read it here?"

"No, son. You don't. Take home with you. Don't worry about the bank account. We've taken care of everything," John said reassuringly.

Fuck. I felt a bit dazed as I walked out to George Square. I crossed the road and sat on a wooden bench, staring at the envelope in my hand. A group of scabby looking pigeons congregated at my feet, as if waiting for me to open it and be done with it. I tore open the envelope and pulled out the letter. For someone as intelligent as dad, his handwriting was fucking shocking. It made me laugh though. I miss the guy so fucking much. And mum too. His letter read:

"Coulter son,

If you're reading this, then I'm dead. And your mother too. I'm so sorry for that. By now, you probably know about our involvement with the Ballaters. We regret ever getting mixed up with them. Once we found out about their true intentions, we tried to break away, but they threatened the lives of your mother and me - what's worse they threatened to kill you. That's why we stayed with them for so long. That, and this – the reason why you're reading this letter today. You have received the information about the Monaco bank account, and you must be wondering why we had one there. There are two reasons, son. The first is obvious: to avoid taxes. The second reason is that this account was used to deposit all the money we skimmed from the many Ballater accounts we administered. The decision to do this was both mine and your mothers and we don't regret it. Not one bit. Empire Properties was just a small part of the Ballaters extensive portfolio. When we realised they would never let us go free, we had two choices: go to the police or steal as much of their money as possible. Going to the police would have put you in danger, so your mother and I decided to rob them blind! She as very clever about it – the Ballaters were unknowingly donating a significant portion of their profits to her charity organizations. It brought her great joy knowing that their ill-gotten gains were being used to help those that needed it the most in Glasgow. The rest of the money we transferred to the bank in Monaco and converted it to gold. Son, there is over one thousand kilograms of gold that now belongs to you. Your mother and I have ensured that you will never lack for anything in life. Our greatest hope is that someday a cure for CIPA will be found, and you can live a normal life. Until then, we want you to be safe and happy. Coulter, spend the money however you like – keep it, give it away, do whatever brings you happiness. We both wish you didn't have to read this letter, but actions have consequences and our dealing (and stealing) has lead to our demise. Please know that you were the greatest gift we ever received and both of us love you so very much.

Stay safe and happy our beloved boy,

Mum and Dad."

A wee old woman with a tartan shopping trolley passed by and stopped to ask, "Are you alright, son?"

I must've looked a fucking mess. I quickly wiped away my tears and asked her to repeat what she said. She explained that she saw me sitting on the bench, reading a letter and crying, and assumed it was a 'Dear John' letter from a lassie. I began to laugh. Fucking laughing and greetin, man. The wee woman encouraged me to keep my spirits up, saying that there's plenty more fish in the sea and a good-looking boy like me won't be single for long. She even joked that if she were younger, she'd be chasing after me herself.

"Nice to see you smiling, son," she said. "Cheery." Her last word as she walked off.

I walked towards the Subway with tears still streaming down my cheeks but a smile on my face. Only in fucking Glasgow can a complete stranger lift you up when you're feeling down. Fucking love this city, man.

1.

After the New Year we moved into the flat at Langside Quay and I have to say it's been fucking amazing. I hadn't realised it but living in my family home with all its memories might not have been the healthiest of choices... But I was fucking grieving – that's my excuse anyway. Not that we moved away from the West End or anything. We haven't. We just spend weekends and some weeknights by the Clyde. Feels like we're on holiday or something. Like we're staying in a hotel. Khaled came round and converted one of the bedrooms into an office cum mini-Base. I thought he'd have to install a bank of severs and lots of electronic shit but he didn't. Just a PC and iMac Pro along with several 4k monitors. He explained that everything was routed through Base in the West End – other than a backup server and hard drive, "Just in case," he said. He knew better than me so I let him get on with it. With the wee Govanhill flat he only set up a laptop. Which was fine because I didn't plan on spending much time there but as Khaled says, "Just in case," I need to be ready for any eventualities. Jasmine had completely redecorated the gaff and it looked fucking fantastic. That girl could easily be an interior decorator if she ever decided to give up the lawyer game. We turned one of the bedrooms into a mini-gym which meant I could get my daily workouts done whenever we stayed there. All in all its was pretty fucking cool man. When I got the all clear from Dr. Assiri, Ken came over to put me through an intense Jiu Jitsu training session. I was expecting the Second-Skin-Suit to make me sweat like a bastard, but it turned out to be super-breathable and infused with silver ions for a cooling effect. Ken asked if I'd be guest of honour at his Jiu Jitsu Youth Clubs showcase competition. I had sponsored it and he wanted me there to hand out trophies and medals and that. Ken was one of five, and I'd fucking do anything for him and his club. They'd recently moved into a new community centre thanks to local funding and charitable donations – my contribution was outfitting their gym with equipment and providing raditional Jiu Jitsu Gi for the kids to wear. I assured Ken that I would be here with Jas by my side.

For the last two weeks Jasmine had been in London. Her old man was unwell and had just been discharged from hospital. COVID 19 man – it's still doing the fucking rounds. With her gone, I was bored and I was tempted to get out and about… If you know what I mean! The scars on my arms had totally healed and being back at training meant I felt fit as fuck. I wasn't ready to face the Ballater's, not yet anyway but I was definitely interested in doing some local crime fighting. With the move to the riverside apartment I'd noticed that after six, the ladies of the night began patrolling Argyle Street and the many streets, roads and alleys off it. I'd read in the Scotsman that businesses' and hotels in the area had complained to the boys in blue about it and the police had been proactive in moving them away from the area. These girls are resilient to say the least, and the fact that many of those who plied their trade on these street were feeding a drug habit meant they had no fucking choice. Not only was my flat close to the so called 'Drag' area but being on the river It was right on the Broomielaw – a well-known place for hookers and their clientele. Look, I'm not against these lassies doing what they have to do. Who the fuck am I to tell someone how to live their life? Nope, that's not fucking me. I feel bad that lassies with drug habits have to do these things and I'm not against them. No fucking way. I'm not a moral crusader out to save them from themselves, but I could help if they were facing problems with punters and that. I mean, these poor girls put their lives at risk every fucking night, selling themselves, and then again when they inject god knows what into their veins. Maybe I could at least kick around… Make sure no one's messing with them and no cunt is trying to murder them and use their fucking skin for a lampshade. Plus the Ballaters are heavily involved in prostitution and drugs. The only way to get street intel is to fucking get out there and pound the pavements. I'd have to be careful though. I mean. It's not just the police I have to watch out for, it's the pimps and the fucking dealers. I'd also have to make sure that the lassies themselves didn't think I was a John looking for a quick shag or even worse, with my West End accent – they might thing I'm an undercover officer or something. Jasmine does her bit for those in need of help at her law office. She doesn't choose the kind of people she helps. She doesn't fucking discriminate – Jas helps everyone. Same with me, just because I don't agree with someone's lifestyle choice doesn't mean that I won't lend a protecting hand, or fist – if some cunt's noising them up. My plan was always to offer my unique services to anyone. Fucking everyone. Rich or poor. It's what mum would've wanted me to do.

Without much of an idea, I began walking along Anderston Quay – cutting up towards Argyle Street on my way to McDonalds. It wasn't late, around seven, and as I got closer to Central Station I began to see more and more women appear on the road. This was where the police try to push the girls up the less well-lit side streets and lanes. They didn't want them selling themselves near the so-called financial district. These darker areas were more dangerous for the lassies. I remember years ago reading that there was a serial killer loose in Glasgow who targeted prostitutes. Don't recall reading anything about him ever being caught – I could be fucking wrong but I think I'm right. Me being just some guy in a hoodie, the lassies I walked past didn't show any interest at all. Their eyes were fixed on the road. Scoping for cars slowing to a kerb crawl.

Packie's old building was nearby, and I smiled, wondering if his girlfriend still lived in the flat and was still on the game. It wasn't all about reminiscing though. Don't know if you remember this but when I was checking out his building and its occupants, I came across a couple of disturbing images of kids on the Dark Web – they weren't too graphic but they linked to a members only website. A quick reverse IP search led me to an address ten floors below Packie's flat, and a username, Toyz4Boyz84. I checked the council database and came up with an Ian MacNeil. Date of birth 3/6/84 – this cunt was defo Toyz4Boyz84 and over the last few days I'd been trying to hack into his computer, but the guy knows a thing or two about security. I'm counting on Khaled to come through with some sort of key, because if I don't gain access to this cunt's network soon, things are going to get messy – for him! I know he's fucking hiding something, and if it's what I suspect then old Toyz4Boyz84 is going to meet his maker soon and I'll tell you this… It aint going to be fucking peaceful!

I'm not a big fan of McDonalds. I fucking hate their burgers but I do like their French fries and the fillet of fish. After the shopping crowds have gone home you get a weird mix of punters coming in for a burger. Folk grabbing a quick bite before or after their work. Guys who might be catching a movie with their bird and don't want to splash the cash on a fancy fucking eatery. Some lonely types who come in for the warmth and the company. Inevitably you'll find a bunch of teenage rockets and dafty's showing off to their pals. You know the type. Wee cunts trying to act hard in front of their girlfriends, noising up the serving staff and that. Most of the time these wee cunts are harmless but not always. Occasionally, one or two of them who think they have something to prove are tooled up with blades. With these bawbags your ordinary citizen has got to be fucking careful. Not me though. I'd take the lot of them on any time of day. Luckily, for them. No one's ever said said a fucking word to me. After finishing my food I retraced my steps back to the flat.

The next night as I walked towards the Hielanman's Umbrella, I heard a voice behind me shout, "Hey mister, ur you the polis?"

Stopping, I turned to face a lassie who looked to be about fucking twelve or thirteen. Her short black hair had patches of white on the fringe and at the sides.

"Do I look like the police?" I said, pulling my facemask down.

"Don't know… Mibbe," she replied and smiled.

"Ur ye lookin fir a girlfriend? I know somedae. Nice lookin. Clean. Cheap tae," she said.

"Shouldn't you be at home doing your homework or something?" I replied.

"Aye right. Ah don't go tae fuckin school. Ave got a job."

"That's good. You have good night now," I said and continued walking.

"Nice tae meet ye officer," she shouted.

I laughed at that. Fucking officer. Pretty fucking funny man. As I crossed the road at York Street, I heard a lassie scream. Looking around, I couldn't see anybody but I heard the scream again – this time louder. I ran like fuck towards it. Halfway down York Street, in the doorway of an office building, a guy had girl by the neck and was punching fuck out of her face. Cunt was so engrossed with what he was doing, he didn't hear me run up behind him. Rather than going for a choke hold, I fucking slapped the guy as hard as I could on the ear. Caught him a total cracker. The pressure from my palm on his eardrum was strong enough to burst the membrane and cause the sharpest of pains. His grip on the lassie loosened, and he turned face me. I went Glasgow old stylee. Fucking nutted him. Right on the bridge of the nose. And I mean hard, like cartilage bone crunching hard. His fucking beak burst open in a crimson wave and he dropped to his knee's not knowing whether to hold his nose or his fucking ear. I considered booting him in the napper but decided to give his other ear an eardrum destroying slap. Totally fucking decked him man. I was about to start booting into his body when the lassie dropped to her knees to protect him.

"Don't hurt him any mer mister, please. He's ma boyfriend. Don't hurt him any mer," she cried.

For fuck sake. A minute ago he was using her pus as a punch bag. Now she's on the ground protecting him.

"He's rattlin mister. Need's some kit. Ave got tae find a couple of punters and he'll be awright. Don't hurt him mister," she pleaded.

The guy was squirming beneath her. I pushed her away and grabbed him by the collar. Fucking blood everywhere.

"I better not see you lift a fucking finger to a woman again," I growled.

The guy couldn't answer me. His ears were in shock and his nose was fucking louping. I let go and his bird tried to help him off the deck. Fuck.

I started feeling sorry for him. The lassie looked like a strong gust of wind would blow her into the Clyde, so I helped the cunt to his feet.

"Am sorry hen," he said. "Am fuckin sorry hen," he was greetin.

I pulled out three twenty quid notes and handed them to the lassie. She didn't know what to say. She kinda just gawped at me then took the cash. Before they left to do whatever the fuck they had to do I told the guy again, "If I see you hitting her again pal. You're fucking dead. "

Both of them crossed the road and disappeared up an alley.

Walking back onto Argyle Street I heard a familiar voice behind me.

"Whit did ye dae that fir?"

It was the young girl from before.

"He was battering his girlfriend. That's not ok," I replied.

She caught up with me and walked by my side as we went under Central Station.

"Naw... ah don't mean that. That cunt deserved a kicking. I mean whit did ye gie her money fir?"

"You saw that did you. Were you following me?" I said pulling down my facemask.

"Naw... I wisnae followin ye pal. Told ye ah thought ye were the polis. Whit did ye gie her money fir?"

"So you weren't following me but you just happened to be behind me as I ran down the street. Are you a stalker," I said and smiled.

"Aye that's right. Am a stalker. Am a fourteen-year-old stalker who stalks auld guys in hoodies."

Old guy. Me? That was too fucking funny man.

"Come on. Tell me. Why did ye gie her money?"

"Felt sorry for her. Her boyfriend was punching her light out for money. I gave her money."

"Aye... That ye did. Efter gien her boyfriend a doin."

We'd reached McDonalds.

"Are you hungry?" I asked.

"Me? Fuckin starvin man," she replied.

I opened the door and guided her in.

"What do you fancy?"

"Me?" she said again. "Big Mac. Large fries. Large Fanta... Please."

"Grab a table then," I said and stood in line for the food.

Returning with the grub I saw she was wiping the table clean with an alcohol wipe.

"Cannae be too careful," she smiled. "Am no wantin Corona again. Fuck that."

Before tucking into her burger and fries she brought out a wee bottle of hand sanitizer and offered me a squeeze. I took of my gloves and she pushed a pea sized drop into my palm. She did the same for herself before grabbing the burger and biting a huge wedge off of it.

She smiled, "Told ye ah wis fucking starvin."

"So, what's your name?" I asked.

"Whit's yours?" she asked.

"I asked first," I smiled. "Coulter. My names Coulter."

"Is that yer first name or yer last?"

She was funny, this lassie.

"First. And yours?"

"Carol," she said with a mouthful of fries.

"Carol but naebday calls me that. The call me Badge."

"Badge? Why do they call you that?"

"Short for Badger," she said pointing to the white patches in her hair.

"It's no dye Coulter. Natural white," she said.

Badger. That's brilliant. I liked that.

"So, Badge. How come you're not at home. Shouldn't you be doing your homework or something?"

"Homework? Ur ye aff yer nut? Me studyin. Ah don't even go tae school. Excluded. Indefinitely," she said, kind of proud like.

"Why are you walking about the Drag. It's not safe. Clearly illustrated by that guy battering his bird," I asked taking a bite of my fish fillet.

"Workin," she said.

Fucking hell man. I just about choked on my food.

'No that kind of work. Am no sellin ma fanny or anythin. I keep the edgy. Ye know – watch oot for the polis and that. Watch oot fir the gangs tae. The lassies gie me money."

Turns out Badge has been on the streets since she was eleven. Her mum battled a heroin addiction for most of her adult life and lost it in the living room of their flat where she overdosed. It was Badge that found her. Worst still her mum walked the streets selling herself and took Badge with her because... Well fuck knows because. After her mums death she went to live with an aunt in Sighthill but her uncle was trying it on with her so she left and she's been in and out of care since. The school exclusion was because of her attendance or her non-attendance, I should say. Fuck me man. If you think your life's fucking shit then you have no idea about what goes on in the streets. I had some idea. What with helping mum with the homeless but man. I lived a charmed fucking life compared to Badge and kids like her. After she finished her McFlurry we walked back out into the Glasgow cold. I had decided to go back to Base and catch up with Khaled to see if he'd found a way to break into Toyz4Boyz84 computer network.

"Right you," I said. "I'm off to the Subway. I've got work to do."

"Me tae," smiled Badge. "Thought ye lived alang the road?" she said pointing along Argyle Street.

"I do," I replied. "It's complicated."

"Well, either ye live alang the road ur ye don't."

"I do and I don't. Like I said, It's complicated... Are you going to be alright?"

"Me? Brand new Coulter. Brand fuckin new."

"Where will you stay tonight? It's fucking freezing Badge."

"Wan ae the lassies lets me crash at hers. Bedsit in Toonhied."

"Ok, well it was nice to meet you. I'll probably see you around,"

"You tae Coulter and thanks fir the scran," she said as she walked off towards the Drag.

On the train back to Kelvinbridge I thought about Badge and her way of life. It's not fucking right. She seemed intelligent and she had a great personality but living the way she does she could be on the highway to fucking heroin hell. Standing on the escalator moving up towards Great Western Road, I decided I was going to help her. How? I had no fucking clue man.

2.

When I spoke to Khaled, he informed me that he'd found a way past Toyz4Boyz84's seemingly impenetrable firewall. He asked me to come by the shop and pick it up. On my way along Great Western Road, I stopped at Myra's Café for a bacon roll and a steaming mug of sweet tea. Badge was still on my mind, and I was unsure of how I could help her. I had to be extra fucking careful as well, considering her age. Some sick cunt's might accuse me of grooming a young lassie or something equally abhorrent. Jas will have some ideas on what we can do, I'm sure of it. Another thought that occupied my mind was what to do with Toyz4Boyz84? The breadcrumbs I discovered on the Dark Web were just the tip of the iceberg. There was no doubt in my mind that the cunt is a pedo. No fucking doubt at all. If you'd seen what I saw you'd fucking agree with me. Guaranteed. I had two options – take matters into my own hands or gather enough evidence and hand him over to the police. Decisions, decisions... Before leaving the café Dr. Manfred gave me a bell about my new health monitoring protocol. It sounded ominous and totally fucking boring.

As usual Khaled was in his workshop and his brother Saleem was dealing with the customers.

"Awright Coulter, ya bawbag," said Saleem as I went through to the back of the shop. My middle finger in the air.

"Coulter my man. How's it hanging," said a smiling Khaled.

"Aye. Fine. You?"

"Never better son. Never fucking better."

"So what have you got for me?" I asked.

He held up what looked like a digital voice recorder.

"This baby I call the Penetrator – with a capital P," he said.

I fucking laughed at that. It sounded like some kind of sex toy or something.

"You couldn't think of a better name man. Fucking thing sounds like a vibrator or something," I said.

"Only to those whose minds are in the gutter," replied Khaled.

"Aye right. Good name for a sex shop though," I laughed. "Tell me how it works."

Khaled explained the capabilities of the Penetrator. It could by pass any network defence, including firewalls, IP spoofing, tracking software, and anti-virus programs – the whole fucking shebang. The beauty of this wee beast is that is that it inserts an applet which acts as a digital key... A fucking untraceable digital key. The cunts you're hacking wont have a fucking scooby that they've been hacked. Man, clever stuff. Fucking Khaled eh? But there was a catch – the hacker had to be within one meter of the network router. Fuck! Unless his router was near his front door, I'd have to gain access to Toyz4Boyz84's flat to initiate the hack. Even if his router was behind his door it'd still be difficult – he most likely had CCTV monitoring his door and surrounding area. Fuck man, every cunt has CCTV these days – it's so fucking cheap to buy. My Kloaker necklace could only hide the top part of my body, leaving my fucking legs on show to anyone. There was no fucking way he'd let me in willingly, and if I forced my way in, he might trigger a delete all files command on his system. I needed a fucking plan. After thanking Khaled, I transferred a Bitcoin payment to his virtual wallet. He didn't even ask why I needed the Penetrator – he simply gave me the device and transferred the necessary software to Base's server.

I was hardly in the house five minutes when Dr Manfred arrived.

"Coulter, we need to talk about your health. In particular your health moving forward," he said all fucking serious like.

"If this is a segue into trying to get me to stop my crime-fighting, then Doc... Don't waste your breath."

"I totally understand where you coming from Coulter, not that I agree but I've been caring for you since your birth. You know you're more than just a patient to me?"

"Getting a bit soft in your old age Doc eh?"

Old Manfred flashed a grin and went over the new health surveillance protocol he wanted me to follow. It wasn't a huge deal, really. He's always so fucking serious. But basically, he wanted me to record my vitals four times a day using an LTE Huawei Watch D that he had even wrapped in gift paper like a big softie. We'd both have access to the Huawei health app on our phones, allowing him to monitor me in real time. If there were any abnormalities, he'd need to administer the Opioid Agonist injection to make me feel pain for about thirty fucking minutes. Once he left, I prepared myself and took the Subway to St Enoch's.

Later on, I was out and about walking towards the Drag.

"Coulter, Coulter," I heard a voice shout from the other side of Argyle Street,

It was Badger, waving like mad and running across the road towards me.

"Hi," I said. "How are you?"

"Aye. Am awright. Look. Ah need yer help... Like noo," she said pointing up towards Blythswood Street.

"A fuckin guy's no wantin tae pay ma pal. He shagged her and he disnae want tae pay. They're fightin," she said running back across the road.

Fuck it, I thought. *Here we go here we go here we fucking go,* I sang to myself as I ran behind Badge – she could fucking run man. I mean she was fast as. Rounding a corner, up an alley, there was a lassie battering fuck out of a guy with her bag. He looked blootered, and he was trying to get away from her but she kept grabbing at him and fucking whacking him one.

"Sandra! Sandra! This is ma pal Coulter. Leave the cunt alone. Coulter will deal wi him," shouted Badge.

Sandra continued to hit the guy demanding her money.

"Sandra, leave him tae Coulter," said Badge again.

"Ah want ma fuckin money from this bastard," Sandra screamed, mad as fuck.

She backed away and the guy turned to Badge and swung at her. Cunt totally missed her as she was too fucking fast. I ran up to him, grabbed his body and tripped onto the deck. He was flailing about like fuck but I wrapped one arm behind his head and grabbed my sleeve and put pressure on his trachea. Sode gurma jime they call it in Jiu Jitsu. Very effective in subduing your opponent. He stopped struggling and eyes rolled in his head.

"Badge, check his pockets," I said.

Badge did as instructed and pulled out a tatty brown leather wallet.

"Take your pals money and add another tenner for her inconvenience."

She pulled out two tenner's and flapped them about.

"It's aw he has," said Badge.

Sandra snatched the money from Badge and was about to boot the guy's head when I stopped her. I let him go and he turned on his side coughing and spluttering.

"I'll make up the rest," I said to Sandra.

The guy was steaming drunk but fucking harmless. I didn't need to hurt him seriously and it was only twenty fucking quid.

"Aye but it's this cunt who should be gien me the money," Sandra screamed, trying to run at the guy lying on the ground.

"Leave him Sandra," said Badge pulling her away and walking her back towards the Drag.

I left the drunk scrambling to his knees and wondering what the fuck had just happened. Catching up with Badge and Sandra, I pulled out a twenty quid note and gave it to her.

"Hod on a minute," said Badge who gave me a wee smirk and ran back to the guy who was now back on his feet but visibly shaken. Badge booted him right in the ball sack and ran back to us laughing.

"He won't dae that again in a hurry," she said. "Fuckin bastard wantin a shag on the cheap," she smiled.

"Whit dis yer pal want me tae dae fir twenty quid?" asked Sandra.

Badge burst out laughing – it made me laugh too.

"Aye you're alright Sandra," I said. "I'm just here to help. The money's yours. No strings."

Sandra put her arm through Badges and they walked ahead of me. On Argyle Street she said her goodbyes telling me I was an absolute fucking gentlemen before she went on her way looking for kerb crawlers.

'Suppose you're hungry?' I asked Badge.

'Aye. Fuckin famished man. Are ye treatin me tae a burger?'

'Of course but I'm going to ask you a favour. Don't worry it's not a big deal. I'll tell you about in Mickey Ds.'

The staff at McDonalds greeted me like I was a fucking regular which was worrying. Nobody batted an eyelid at Badge. My guess is that if she walked into a shop or whatever the folk there would be watching her like a hawk, worried she'd knock something.

"So whit's this favour ye want?" Badge asked as she slurped an extra-large diet coke.

"I need help hacking a guys computer," I replied with a smile.

"How can ye no dae it yerself?"

"It's complicated," I said.

"Complicated how?"

Fuck it. I had no choice but to tell her all about me finding Toyz4Boyz84 on the Dark Web and that I suspected he was a pedo who could be selling photos and videos of kids been abused.

"Am fuckin in," she said. "Whit dae have tae dae?"

"If this guy is who I think he is... I need you to get as close to his network router as possible and flip this switch. Thirty seconds is all you need. Means you have to get inside his flat," I said showing her the Penetrator – didn't tell her its name though for obvious fucking reasons.

"Piece ah piss Coulter. Piece ah fuckin piss. When?" she asked all confident like.

"Listen, I'm not saying it'll be dangerous... But I'll be on the stair, and if you're not out in five minutes flat... I'll kick the fucking door down."

"Coulter dae ye know how long ave been on the streets. Ah can fuckin handle maself. When dae ye want tae dae it?"

"What about now?" I said.

"Let's get goin then ya big fanny," she smiled.

We walked out into the Glasgow night and of course it started pishing it down. Central station sheltered us for a wee while whilst we discussed the plan. We'd head up to Toyz4Boyz84 flat. Badge would chap the door all innocent like and ask if her pal Mary was there. She said she'd use her charms and get the guy to let her in. I told her I'd be right behind her in the shadows on the stairs.

When we got to the building the Concierge didn't even give us a second look. He buzzed us in when we told him we were pals of Ian. In the lift I gave Badge the Penetrator, and I got off on the floor beneath Toyz4Boyz84, and creeped up the stairs just out of view. I heard Badge knock his door and after a while it opened.

"Oh hi," said Badge. "I'm lookin fir Mary. Is she in?"

"There's nae Mary here hen. Do one," said Toyz4Boyz84.

"Ur ye sure? She told me she wis seein a guy. I thought it wis you."

"There's nae Mary here hen. Sorry," the cunt tried to close the door.

"Is there any chance ah could use yer bog mate? Am burstin. Please. It's pissin it doon ootside and am fuckin drenched. Jist five minutes of heat. Please," said Badge.

Toyz4Boyz84 hesitated and then said, "Aye. Ok. Just five minutes then."

The door closed and Badge was inside. I checked my Huawei watch and got ready to fucking ram the place should I have to. Man, talk about a long five minutes. Felt like a fucking hour, more even. On the six-minute mark I was about to barge through the stair door when I heard voices and a door opening.

"Listen mister. Thanks for lettin me use yer toilet. Am sorry tae huv put ye oot. Whit's yer name anyway," she asked.

"Ian," said Toyz4Boyz84.

"Well thank you Ian. Am glad Mary wisnae here. Am glad ah got tae meet ye. Can ah come back sometime. Ye know... If ah need the loo?" smiled Badge enticingly.

"Aye. Aye ye can. Anytime yer welcome."

"Yer ah real gentleman Ian. Ah mean that," said Badge as she headed for the lift.

I almost pished myself laughing at her acting man. Fuck, if they ever wanted to film a Glaswegian version of Lolita... Badge would pass the audition with flying colours.

Jumping down the stairs I waited at the lift. When the door opened a smiling Badge greeted me and handed back the Penetrator.

"See. Ah told ye. Fuckin piece ah piss," she said.

"Brilliant. What did you see inside?" I asked.

"The place wis a fuckin tip. Don't think he's got a maid service," she laughed. "The bog wis just by his bedroom. He shut the door quick like. Stood ootside whilst ah pretended tae pee. Ah did whit ye telt me tae dae. Thirty seconds."

"You're a star Badge. Have you ever considered a career in acting? I think you'd be excellent?"

"Me? Actin? Aye right," she laughed.

As we strolled back along Argyle Street towards the Drag, the rain let up. Badge wanted to know what I was going to do about Toyz4Boyz84, and I told her I wasn't exactly sure – that was the fucking truth. I originally thought about just killing the cunt – if I found incriminating evidence of course. I mean, I'm not a total psycho! Anyway, I told Badge I'd talk to Jasmine if I found pedo stuff on his computer. You know... Go down the legal route – not the murder route. Sandra got out of a motor on the Drag. Badge said she'd see me later and ran towards her pal. I didn't even have time to give her some money for helping me out. I shouted I'd see her later, and I continued towards St Enoch's and the train back to Base.

3.

After returning to the warmth of Base, I turned on my computer and hacked my way into Toyz4Boyz's network and hard drives. Kind of wished I hadn't though. There was literally thousands upon thousands of pedo porn images and videos. This cunt had set up a members-only page on the Dark Web, using a peer-to-peer system to buy and swap these illegal materials. With a constantly running IP spoofing program, it would be nearly impossible to trace his IP address. However, I knew where he lived, so that wasn't a big issue for me. What I was more interested in were the IPs of the other members. I bet you a thousand quid most of them weren't as cautious as Toyz4Boyz84 and let me tell you, there loads of fucking members, many of whom were in Glasgow – sick fucking bastards. I called Jas for advice and told her I wanted to make the biggest impact possible. She warned me that if I submitted what I found anonymously to the police they might ignore it. Plus some of the IPs could belong to policemen or people with clout like politicians and that. Fuck, that kind of thing hadn't even crossed my mind. Jas suggested sending all the info to Dale Martin at the Evening Times, an investigative journalist who wasn't afraid to stir the shit, especially if the shit involves important people. Jas had his personal email which she forwarded to me. I told her I missed her, and she surprised me by saying she'll be home tomorrow which was good fucking news. Meant her old man must be a lot better.

The Next day, Big Gerry picked me up and took me across the water to the Southside. It was Ken's Youth Club Jiu Jitsu do and I was the guest of honour. Which was pretty fucking funny. Don't get me wrong, I was chuffed to be the one handing out the awards and that but after my dealings with Cammy Ballater and his crew, I wasn't exactly a bastion of moral turpitude – hardly a good fucking role model. On the way to Queens Park, I broached the subject of what to do with what I found on Toyz4Boys84 computer with the big man.

"Hold on Coulter, hold the fuck on," he said. Turning down Glen Campbell and his Wichita Linesman. Shit, if he's turning down the music you know he's really pissed off.

"You're telling me that you hacked some cunts computer and found shitloads of kiddie porn and you're asking me what to do about it?"

"Aye, big man. That's exactly what I'm asking."

"That's an easy discussion. Fucking end him. Pedo bastard doesn't deserve to be breathing good Glasgow air."

"That was my first thought and all big man, but I spoke to Jas," I said.

"What did she have say about it?"

"Let's just say her idea didn't include any fucking violence," I smiled.

"Look its just not one cunt. It's a fucking network of them. Jas said take everything I've got, all the evidence and share it with Dale Martin."

"What? The guy from the Times?"

"Aye. She said he'd publicise it and print the IP addresses of all the pedos. Jas was worried that some of them might be police. If I sent it to St Andrew's Square it might get 'lost' if you know what I mean."

"She's fucking right you know. Jas's smart. What the fuck she's doing with you I've no clue," he laughed.

"Bawbag," I replied with a grin. "I'm going to contact Dale, but I want to fuck up Toyz4Boyz too. Can't off him though. Jas would be annoyed."

"What are you thinking? A doing? If it was me I'd cut his balls off and stuff them down his throat."

"Haven't decided yet. I like the balls idea though."

Arriving at the Youth Club, I asked to Gerry to join me. Ken had never met the big man but he knew about him. His smiling face greeted us at the door. Gerry and Ken exchanged a firm handshake.

"Come inside, lads," he said. "Coulter, I thought Jasmine was coming? Not that I'm not pleased to meet Gerry... It's just Jas would class up the place."

"Aye. I know what you mean. She's still down south with her folks. Next time Ken... I'll make sure she comes."

"Let's me show were your money's went," Ken smiled.

"It was just some Jiu Jitsu stuff for the kids, Ken. No big deal," I replied.

"Always modest. Just some stuff for the kids, he says. Wait until you see the gym," Ken grinned.

He opened double doors, revealing a brand-new games hall. This was no fucking gym, man. There was room enough for fixed weight gear, five aside football, basketball, netball, badminton and table tennis. Everything you could think of was here – a fully functioning sports centre. Mum would've been ecstatic if she saw what her and dad's money helped create. There were chairs set up and a long table adorned with shiny trophies, medals, and ribbons. Half the floor was covered in mats and soon enough, proud parents filled the room as their children displayed their newfound martial arts skills. The big man and I sat as guests of honour at the front, while Ken took on the role of MC for the event. After the younger kids showcased their talents, Ken introduced two girls and two boys, probably around sixteen or so. Instead of Jiu Jitsu moves, these fit teenagers performed something called Tricking. I'd never heard of it before, but man... What the actual fuck? According to Google, 'Tricking flawlessly blends martial arts, gymnastics, and dance into a breath-taking display.' Man, these youngsters defied gravity with their fitness levels, and it was fucking awesome to watch. Afterwards, I asked Ken if there was any way for me to learn some of those moves. It would not only look impressive on the streets, but also give me an edge over potential attackers. Ken was more than happy to oblige and told me that Wednesday nights were dedicated to Tricking and I had an open invite. Fucking magic man.

Before he dropped me off at Base the big man said I needed help in fucking up some pedos, he was my man. Told him I'd phone if I needed his particular skillset.

4.

After some quick consideration, I agreed with Jas's suggestion to send the pedo network info to Dale Martin. It may not bring all of them justice, but at least it'd be exposed to the public eye. Name and shame the cunts. However, I couldn't resist the urge to inflict some serious fucking pain along with the name and shame, and my sick twisted mind came up with a brilliant idea which I'll get into later. Lets just say, Toyz4Boyz84 would be losing some of his toys! Before anything else, I had to reach out to Dale. I chose to do this anonymously until we established a connection and I could confirm his trustworthiness. Setting up an untraceable anonymous email was a piece of piss. I sent him a cryptic message to gauge his interest and within five minutes he responded, wanting to know who I was. I told him I was just a concerned citizen tired of seeing our city's reputation ruined by predator cunts. I wanted to make the streets safer for everyone. Then, I mentioned the Ballater Boys and how they think they can get away with anything. And just for fun, I hinted that I was responsible for Cammy Ballater's grim demise, not a rival gang. Dale was persistent and wanted to know how I discovered the pedo network, so I told him about my unrestricted access to the Dark Web and stumbling upon Toyz4Boyz84. He was eager for more details; he knew it would make for a fucking great story – exposing a complex paedophile network. I promised evidence and teased him with a taste of what I had in store. But for my plan to work, I'd need Badge's help again.

As I geared up for my night-time adventure, I received a delivery from the boys at Shenzhen Fabrications, courtesy of Dr. Manfred's clinic. I'd been eagerly waiting for this wee beauty for fucking weeks, and when I finally opened the box and held it in my hand, it looked even better than the renders I'd received from China. The Hummingbird 1.0 was a micro RPAS device – essentially a drone for those unfamiliar with the term Remotely Piloted Aircraft System. But this wasn't just any old DJI type drone. The Hummingbird was a feat of modern science, man. It may have been small, but it was built to fucking last with its graphene and titanium construction. It's advanced battery could last an hour, though you only got forty minutes of flight time due to its return-to-home safety feature. And lets not forget the onboard sensors, which took this puppy to the next level. With its 4k camera and night vision capabilities, along with its Sonar-FLIR photoimaging system that could see through walls, and collision avoidance sensors that made it damn near impossible to crash – unless I was steaming drunk, of course! And as if that weren't enough, it also had next-gen A.I. smarts with Chat GPT-6 Plus technology and satellite connectivity to communicate with SkyeEye. Oh, and did I mention there was a fancy app for my Pixel to control it? Just in case someone tried to knock it or if it somehow managed to crash, the solid-state hard drive would self-destruct along with all its sensors – not that I wanted that happen after shelling out a fucking King's ransom for it. Despite my excitement to try it out, I needed to charge it first and find a secluded area so I could learn how to operate it properly. Once I dealt with Toyz4Boyz84, I'd make some time for flying lessons.

On the Subway to St Enoch's, I went over the plan to deal with our neighbourhood pedo. My trusty Eraser Taser was going to assist – I'd need the help of Badge too and I hoped she'd be on or near the Drag. It was only eight o'clock but there was a number of kerb crawlers already out scouting for fanny. There was no sign of Badger. Walking towards my flat a private taxi pulled up and out came Badge and her pal Sandra who thanked me again for helping her the other night. She said she'd see Badge later and crossed the road where an old guy in a Jag picked her up. It was then I noticed Badger had a fucking black eye. She tried to conceal it with make-up but under the yellow of the streetlight it was fucking obvious someone had smacked her a stoater.

"What happened to you?" I asked.

"You mean this?" she said pointing at her eye.

"Who hit you?"

"It's nothin Coulter. Jist some guy."

"What guy Badge? When did it happen?"

"Last night. It wis wan ae they SV cunts. Tryin tae get me tae work fir them," she said.

"SV? Who the fuck is that?" I asked.

"Skal Vac. Fucking eastern European mafia. Them cunts run a brothel and a lot of the street lassies."

"What? They wanted you to work in a brothel. Badge you're not even sixteen. You need to be careful,"

"Don't worry aboot me Coulter. Them cunts wont catch me. I'm too quick fir them."

"Yeah but your eye... Not fucking quick enough," I smiled.

"Forget aboot them bawbags. Are ye going to McDonalds? I only had a bowl ae cornflakes at Sandra's. Wi her habit she's not a regular shopper at Aldi."

"Aye, no bother but first I'm going to need a wee favour again. There's money in it," I said.

"Fuck yer money man. I'll help ye. Fir you Coulter... My services are free," she laughed.

Toyz4Boys84's building loomed ahead as we made our way towards it and I told Badge my plan. She was all for helping me rid Glasgow of its pedos. We walked into the foyer, where a different concierge was on duty than last time. Badge spun him some story about visiting her cousin Ian, and he buzzed us in without question. As before, she knocked on his door and pretended to be visiting him. This time, however, I gave her the Eraser Taser set to close contact stun mode, which would deliver a 2000-volt shock without deploying a Limpet Bullet. I told Badge to use it on the cunt as soon as she got inside. I didn't want to risk kicking down the door and triggering any data wiping mechanisms he might've set up. Badge's eyes lit up when she saw the ET – she was ready for action.

"Whit ye daein aw this fir Coulter?" she asked in the lift. "Ye know, helpin the lassies on the street an' that. Dealin with this fucking pedo bastard. I mean. Whit ur ye daein it aw fir?"

The lift chimed as it reached the floor below Toyz4Boyz84's flat. With a grin, I stepped out and said, "Why not?" as the doors closed behind me and the lift continued on to the next floor. I quietly made my way up the stairs and waited. Badge chapped the door and I heard her say "Hi, remember me? Ah wis in the area and thought ah'd gie ye a visit." As soon as she was inside his hallway, she fucking tazed the cunt. Within seconds of entering, she shouted for me to come in. From my backpack I produced a roll of gaffa-tape and some zip-cuffs. Toyz4Boyz84 was lying on the deck in a pool of his own piss, completely fucking dazed man. After closing his front door, I asked Badge to help me move the tub of shit to his bedroom. With his hands cuffed and his mouth taped shut with gaffa tape, we took a closer look around. His bedroom was a fucking mess. It reeked of sweat and spunk. I warned her not to touch anything as I pulled out a hammer and three steel spikes from my bag. The first spike went into the top of his bedroom door, while the other two were hammered into each bottom corner. With Badge's help, we got Toyz4Boyz84 on his feet and I raised his arms above his head, securing them to spike with the zip-cuff. Then we spread the cunts legs and attached one zip-cuff to each ankle, fastening them to the bottom spikes. Fear filled Toyz4Boyz84's eyes as he realized that this may be the end of his paedophiliac ways. I asked Badge to wait outside the flat while I retrieved the ET and prepared to carry out my plan.

"Whit ye gonnae dae wi the cunt. Ah want tae watch," she said.

"No you don't. Get outside and be ready to phone 999 like I told you," I replied.

Reluctantly she did as I asked but gave me the middle finger as she left. I pulled the tape from the fucker's mouth.

"Whit ur daein mister," he said. "Listen, ye've got the wrang guy," he spluttered.

"Doubt that," I said as I pulled my shiny new serrated hunting knife from my waist.

"Whit ye gonnae dae wi that mister. Please there's been a mistake. It's no me yer efter," the cunt was bubbling.

"Toyz4Boyz84 ring any bells?" I asked. His face went pure white.

Taping his gub shut, I then pulled the CCTV DVR from the wall and shot a limpet bullet into it totally fucking melting the hard drive and all the footage. I turned back to him and said, "By accident I found out what you've been doing. Not just you ya cunt. Your whole fucking network and I just want you to know... I'm going to take great pleasure in doing this."

I reached into my pocket and pulled out two elbow-length disposable gloves, the kind used during autopsies. Toyz4Boyz84 eyes pleaded with me – I ignored the cunt. With a swift movement, I pulled down his crispy keks, revealing piss-stained boxers. With my knife at the ready, I grabbed him by the balls and used the knife to slice open his scrote and carve off his testicles. His screams of agony were muffled by the tape, and a waterfall of blood ran down his legs. He struggling like a bastard, screaming bloody murder but I hadn't fucking finished. I pulled away the tape and pushed his nads into his mouth. Cunt resisted, but eventually opened his mouth to fully receive his own body parts. I taped his mouth shut tight. Grabbing the ET I switched it to a lower voltage close contact stun and pressed hard against the mushy area were his balls once hung. I fucking pushed up hard and pulled the trigger, and the bastard danced about like a fucked-up marionette. The excessive heat generated by the ET cauterised his wound and stemmed the flow of blood. The door he was hanging from looked like it might give way any minute, and old Toyz4Boyz84 looked like he had two gobstoppers in his gub. Discarding the gloves and wiping my weapons on his shirt, I packed up everything into my backpack and made an exit. As I left, I casually mentioned that an ambulance and the police were on their way. Just as expected, the bedroom doors hinges gave way and the dirty pedo bastard smashed on to the floor – face fucking first. A perfect end to a perfect night of revenge.

Badge and I got in the lift and I handed her a burner phone, telling her to call the police to report that somebody attacked her boyfriend.

"Give me an award-winning performance," I smiled.

Dialling 999 she frantically told the emergency operator what had happened and where she was. "Send the polis now and a fucking ambulance…"

I could only clap my hands at her BAFTA winning acting. She handed the phone back and gave me a curtsey. Before leaving the building she pointed out the blood stains on my tracksuit. Fuck! I thought I'd managed to avoid the splatter but obviously not. We both waved to the concierge as we exited the front entrance. The sound of police sirens approached, and we calmly walked away in the direction of Lancefield Quay.

"I'll need to scoot to my flat to change out of these blood-soaked trousers then we can hit McDonalds," I said.

"Where's yer flat Coulter? How come ah always see ye goin tae the underground?" Badge asked.

"You want to come up and wait whilst I get quick wash and a change," I said pointing to my building.

"Whit the fuck Coulter. You live there? You must be fuckin minted man."

It was pretty funny when I let her into the apartment and put on the lights. She really couldn't believe I stayed in a penthouse.

"Make yourself comfy Badge. I'll only be ten minutes," I said and went to shower and change into a new tracksuit.

When I'd finished I found Badge out on the balcony.

"Some fuckin view ye've got from here Coulter. The city looks beautiful from this height. Not so much from the fuckin street though," she smiled.

"That's why I bought it. For the views," I winked.

"Whit? Ye own this place? Yer no rentin?"

"It's mine," I said. "Well, it mine and Jasmine's. My girlfriend."

'It's some place right enough. Yer bird's lucky tae huv a guy like you," she said.

'When you meet her. Try not to say she's my bird," I replied with a smile. Badge laughed at that and we went back out into the night to get our McDonalds fix. If you thought what we did, or should I say... What I did to Toyz4Boyz84 would put us off our food. You were wrong – we were Lee Marvin man!

After finishing our meal, Badge and I walked to St Enoch's. I told her about having a place in the West End and promised to introduce her to Jas. Before I went down the escalator, Badge asked me again why I doing what I do - helping folk and that. I told her I'd tell her all about it... One day! As I descended to the station I called out for her to stay safe. But deep down, I felt guilty about leaving her to walk the dangerous streets alone – earning money by keeping an eye out for the police and staying with her prostitute friend who was struggling with a smack addiction. I fucking have to do something to help her man; it can't just be about fighting and causing bodily harm. If I truly want to make a difference and help those that need it most, violence can't be my only solution. Can it?

5.

Upon arriving back at Base, I quickly fired off all the IP address info
to Dale Martin. I also informed him about Toyz4Boy84's unfortunate
ball-less situation. It was now his turn to do what he does best. He
thanked me and asked for a meet up in person. I replied with a
noncommittal "maybe." Later on, I called Jas and told her about meeting
Badger and how she helped me deal with the pedo bastard. I also told
her that I really wanted to help Badge in some way but admitted I
didn't have fucking clue how. Jas said she'd think about it, and after
we hung up, I went online to research Skal Vac, the mysterious gang
Badger had mentioned. Turns out they are a highly organised crime
syndicate operating in Montenegro and Serbia, known for their lucrative
involvement in drug and human trafficking. They're tentacles stretch
across western Europe and they're heavily involved with certain South
American drug cartels. They're money-making interests are vast – they
are one of the biggest seller's of cocaine and it's derivatives, and these
cunts are the biggest traders in women for prostitution. That's how Badge
knew about them. Funny thing is though, I couldn't find any info about
them having a presence in Glasgow which was fucking strange. An online
search of the newspapers yielded fuck all. I'd need to track down Badge
and gather more info from her.

It was Dr Manfred ringing my doorbell that woke me out of an odd
dream. I'd stayed up late trying to gather as much intel as I could on the
Skal Vac mob. If they really were operating within the city boundaries
then I was going to have to fuck with them somehow.

"Late night was it," said old Manfred as I opened the door.

"Kind of," I smiled as I let him in.

"Was it your handiwork I read about in today's Daily Record?"

Fuck... I didn't think Dr Manfred read our daily tabloid.

"Not sure what you're talking about. I had a quiet night last night," I
smiled.

"So the castration of a paedophile wasn't your handiwork?"

"Me? I know nothing about it. I'll check it out online later though."

"I believe you. Thousands wouldn't," he smiled. "But... There was a notable spike in your vitals for a short period last night. Remember I'm tracking you with the Huawei Health app."

"Probably when I went out for a jog," I winked.

I was surprised to see Toyz4Boyz84 and his emasculated state plastered across the morning headlines. It was clear that the reporter must have been closely monitoring police communications, as they got the Anderston scoop in record time. No doubt some money had exchanged hands for this exclusive story. Dale Martin's story about the pedo network was far more important and all I had to do was cool my heels until it was published in the Evening Times. Dr. Manfred wanted to check my bloods and drew some of my red stuff to send to the lab. After a quick check of my vitals he left for the clinic and I immediately went online, sending Dale an email, asking him when the story would likely be out – his reply stated that he was doing his due diligence and checking the accuracy of the info I'd supplied. If the Times legal team ok'd it – the story would run soon. Fucking cool man. I could hardly wait to read about those pedo cunts getting their doors kicked in by the boys in blue. As the evening approached, I squeezed my body into my Second-Skin-Suit and pulled on a pair of trackie bottoms and my hoodie. Jas called to say she'd arrived at Glasgow Airport and she'd see me soon. My girl had come up with an idea on how we could help Badge. Jas was smart man – a lot fucking smarter than me. Her suggestion was to have Badge tutored by Val; my former home-school teacher. It was an excellent idea though normally, Val taught folk in their house. No fucking problem, she can teach Badge here. Of course, I still needed to ask Badge if she wanted my help. Who knows? She might tell me to fuck off. After hanging up. I popped in my XM5 earbuds and played some music on my walk to the Subway. Cant fucking believe I'm admitting this, and I totally blame it on big Gerry. An American lassie called

Deanna Carter – a fucking country singer man, sung me to the train station. I'll play some Tool later. You know, just to even it up a bit!

Sitting opposite me on the Subway train was a woman with her child. The kid must've been about three or four. Very cute. I pulled down my facemask and made funny faces at her. She was giggling like fuck. Her mum was looking at me and looking at her kid. Soon all three of us were laughing – it was funny as. They waved to me when they got off at Cowcaddens. It suddenly occurred to me that if the mum knew what I'd been up to last night, I wonder if she would've been so friendly. Not that it bothered me because, I guarantee, if she saw what I saw on that cunt Toyz4Boyz84's computer she'd have grabbed the fucking knife from my hand and cut his balls of without a bye or leave. Did I feel any guilt about what I did? Did I fuck, and I'd do it again in a heartbeat. The thing with CIPA, apart from not feeling pain is that it has dulled my emotions. Not totally but it has... That's the honest truth. For example I don't feel fear at all. Fuck, if I did I wouldn't be able to do what I'm fucking doing. There's no remorse either – the CIPA threw that baby out with the bath water. Love is there, obviously. I loved... Love mum and dad. And Jasmine man. I'm fucking mad about her. I really am. Empathy's there too. I feel it. It's dulled but it's there – in my heart and in my fucking soul.

It was still early when I got out of St Enoch's. Badge would show up later, so I took a wander down Jamaica Street towards the riverbank. Don't know what the fuck it is about water but it relaxes your mind. As I walked along the Broomielaw, I couldn't help but wonder when the pedo story would make the front page of the Evening Times. Should've checked the newsagents when I came out of the Subway. Eventually, I made my way to the Drag, hoping to find Badge. But she was nowhere to be seen. I was considering going to Lancefield Quay when I spotted Sandra, the lassie that Badge lives with. I waved at her and ran across the road to talk to her. She was full of it and I could barely get a fucking word out of her. She told me Badge had been giving cheek to a couple of guys and they bundled her into a van. Fuck sake. Sandra said it happened last night, probably not long after I fucking left her. When I asked if she had any idea where they could've taken Badge, she told me to fuck off as she was looking for punters. My mind was racing a mile a fucking minute. Could it be the same cunts who gave her the black ye? The Skal Vac mob? Fucking hell man. Without wasting a second I bolted towards Central Station when suddenly, the lassie I helped a few nights ago appeared from a side street. I ran over to speak to her.

"Hi," I said. "Remember me?"

She looked like she was rattlin a bit.

"Aye... Aye ah dae. Ma memories no that bad," she said.

"I'm looking for Badger. Her pal Sandra says she saw her being pushed into a van last night. Do you know anything about it?"

"Naw mate," she said. "But if it's them SV cunts. The wans that punched her. They'll huv her at the City Centre."

"What do you mean the City Centre?" I asked.

"The fuckin City Centre Hotel. It's a knocking shop these guys run."

My heart was fucking pounding. Badge, kidnapped and in a fucking brothel.

"Where the fuck is this place?"

"Richard Street. Ye cannae miss it."

A black taxi passed and I jumped it. I had to get back to Base and get my fucking gear. On the way I phoned the big man and told him to get to my bit ASAP. Then I Googled the City Centre Hotel. Nothing. Sweet fuck all. Fuck! Remember earlier when I told you about not feeling fear? Well currently I was feeling something like fucking fear. Not for myself for Badge. When I reached Base, I grabbed my backpack, the Eraser Taser, the Hummingbird RPAS and the hunting knife I castrated Toyz4Boysz84 with. A horn beeped outside and it was big Gerry. I dived in the front seat and told him to get to Richard Street as fast as he fucking could.

"Who put a red-hot poker up your arse?" asked Gerry.

"It's a long fucking story big man," I said. "But the jist of it is that a bunch of cunts have a fourteen-year-old lassie in knocking shop."

"What the fuck? Who?"

"Have you heard of the Skal Vac mob?" I asked.

"The eastern European mafia? Of course I've fucking heard of them. Who hasn't?"

"Me. I'd never fucking heard of the cunts until Badge told me about them."

"Badge? Who the fuck's Badge?" Gerry asked.

"She's the lassie. The fourteen-year-old. Her nicknames Badger because of her hair."

As succinctly as possible, I told the big man what I'd been up to over the last few days. Before long we were at one end of Richard Street. It was fucking empty apart from a black Mercedes parked outside an old building. We waited and watched. Soon enough two jet black Transit vans appeared and a bunch of guys got out, waited outside the door for a minute and then went inside.

"I don't want to get too close big man. It might give the game away," I said, pulling the Hummingbird from my backpack.

"Check this out Gerry,"

With a simple flick of a switch, the Hummingbird was ready for take-off. I pulled out my Pixel and opened the controller app, knowing this would be its first flight since I didn't have any time to practice beforehand. As I rolled down the car window, I put my hand with the drone in my palm outside and pressed the launch button on the app. The small but powerful device quickly ascended into the air, its 4k camera capturing everything in its view as it flew towards the building ahead. It seemed like an old structure, possibly a former merchants office. Above the entrance were two CCTV cameras. On the metal front door was a Ring fucking doorbell. I manoeuvred the Hummingbird up to the windows of the first floor, but they were completely boarded up and offered no glimpse inside. Switching to sonar-FLIR mode, I could detect a lot of movement on different floors – likely folk getting their hole. The top floor appeared empty, with no sign of activity. Flying over to the back of the building, I switched to 4k with night vision. There was a metal fire escape running up the building, each of the four floors had a fire exit. Small CCTV camera's above each of these doors emitted a red pulsing light. At the fire exit on the top floor, I took advantage of the Hummingbird's small size and almost silent operation to focus is camera on the door lock. Fucking thing looked like a manual mechanism, my sov ring would be useless, but that would be my point of entry for sure. I'd have to be fucking quick though because my Kloaker necklace would only hide half my body and I didn't want any of the cunts inside to have advance notice of my entry. Engaging the Return to Home function, the drone gracefully returned to my open palm.

"Right bawbag. What's the plan?" asked the big man.

"Turn round and head to the alley behind the building," I said.

Gerry reversed and swung the motor round, but to our fucking disappointment there was no entrance to the alley. Just a sizable metal gate with security cameras on either side. Fuck sake.

"Right," I said pulling the ET and hunting knife from my backpack. "Looks like I'm going in alone."

"Fucking risky Coulter," said Gerry "You don't even know if the lassies is there or not and you don't know how many SV cunts could be inside."

"No other option big man. Keep your mobile handy, and don't worry I'll be stealthy like a black fucking panther," I grinned, pulling up my facemask and getting out of the car.

With the ET and knife secured to my waist, I made a run towards the gate. If any cunt was monitoring the CCTV cam all they'd see was a pair of trackie wearing legs climbing over it. I'd have to be quick though, so I made like fucking Spiderman and jumped on to the gate, which was shoogly as fuck, and it made a bit of a racket as I scaled it. Luckily, I'm pretty fucking fit so climbing it was a piece of piss. I landed in some tall grass and waited a few seconds to see if anyone noticed me.

Nothing. I moved forward. Should've brought a torch as it was fucking dark. I pulled out my Pixel and saw that there was a crumbling brick wall to climb – two walls later and I was at the fire escape. Pressed against the wall, I carefully climbed up the rusting metal steps. With Kloaker activated I was damn near invisible. Outside the top floor fire exit, I pulled out my knife and began jemmying the lock. It clicked open and I snuck inside. No alarm, thank fuck. I was in a dark corridor, ahead was a bar of light sneaking up the stairs from the floor below. Sex noises could be heard as I made it to the top of the stairs. This is where things could get fucking tricky man. I put away the knife and pulled out the Eraser Taser with its kill-switch engaged, ready for any fucking threat. Like a cat in the night, I descended the stairs slowly, the sound of sex got louder. A voice speaking a foreign language crackled over a walkie-talkie somewhere nearby. At the last step, I paused and took a deep breath before stepping into the dimly lit corridor. A guy standing outside one of the rooms didn't see me at first, giving me enough time to aim and shoot a Limpet Bullet into his left eye, causing his dome to implode. Fucking gruesome and awesome at the same time. As the cunt tumbled to the deck, I quickly grabbed his walkie-talkie. Just as I was about to continue down the stairs, I heard a familiar voice coming from behind the door the guy had been guarding – it was Badge. Pressing my ear against the door, I could hear muffled screams and the sound of a struggle. A male voice shouted, "Hold still ya wee bitch. This is gonnae hurt you mer than me." With twist of the doorknob, the door clicked opened. The guy was too busy with Badge to hear me sneaking in. The ET was replaced by my knife. The cunts trousers were at his knees and Badge was face down on the edge of a bed. He was pulling at her jeans.

"Huv ye ever hud it in the arse hen," he said.

I fucking pounced man. My left arm hooked around his neck and had him in a choke hold.

I whispered in his ear, "Have you ever had it up the arse pal," and with one swift thrust, the knife went right up his fucking shitehole. His grip on Badge loosened immediately, and I turned the knife in a one eighty. My hand stretched over his mouth. Cunts eyes looked like they were going to pop out their fucking sockets. "Badge, its me. Come on," I ordered as I did another one eighty turn with the blade. She looked dopey. The Skal Vac mob must've drugged her. She kind of just stood there staring at me and the guy.

"Badge... We are leaving... Now!"

The guys knees gave up the ghost. I lowered him to the floor and watched as he shit liquid red. Badge stood looking down at him. With my trainer firmly on his windpipe he was losing consciousness along with buckets of arse blood. I helped Badge pull her jeans up and her t-shirt down. I needed to be quick just in fucking case, so I left the cunt semi-lifeless, grabbed Badge and dragged her to the door. I waited a second or two before pulling her into the corridor where she nearly tripped over the dead guard and pushed her towards the stairs to the top floor.

"Coulter," she slurred. "Is that you?"

"Aye. It's me. You're ok now Badge. You're safe, but we need to be quiet and get up the stairs," I said.

The corridor had three other rooms, and judging by sounds coming from them, they were fucking occupied. At the stairs, I fireman lifted Badge and bombed it up. At the top of the fire escape, I phoned the big man and told him to meet me at the other side of the alley. There was no way Badge could climb over those brick walls and gate. Creeping down the metal stairs, I heard the sound of men shouting. Fuck, some cunts found the bodies. I lowered Badge to her feet and pushed her downstairs and got the ET ready. You know... Just in fucking case. Fucking thought we'd made and all. I really did until the second-floor fire door burst open, and before I could do a thing, I heard the loudest bang and fucking battering ram struck my chest. Everything appeared to move in slow motion. The blast had jolted Badge out of her stupor, and she staggered down towards the bottom of the fire escape. Me? Me... I was looking at a guy holding a sawn-off shotgun – cunt was smiling and I was flying over the guard rail. I'd taken both barrels right in the fucking chest. Time speeded up and I descended like a ton of bricks. The ground was surprisingly hard. The wind was totally knocked out of me as I lay there for a millisecond looking up towards the night sky, not knowing if it was New York or New fucking Year. Above me, the guy was leaning over the guard rail, loading two shells into the shotgun. He was still smiling as he snapped it shut and took aim at me on the deck. Fucking lucky I was still holding the Eraser Taser and instinct took over – I fired, and the Limpet Bullet hit him under his chin, imploding the bottom half of his face. He dropped to his knees; the shotgun went off and the rest of his napper sprayed crimson into the night as it was torn apart by hundreds of lead pellets. Badge's face appeared in front of me. Her eyes wider than before. Her adrenaline counteracting whatever fucking drug they'd given her.

"Coulter, Coulter!" she said. "Ur ye awright?"

"Brand new," I smiled. "Help me up and let's get the fuck out of here."

Badge pulled me to my feet, and both of us staggered towards the other end of the alley. Instead of a wall, a big wire fence blocked our way. At the corner there was a curled opening which we slipped through. Behind us we heard the sound of guys shouting as we made it to the road. Big Gerry appeared, and both of us dived in the back seat of his motor.

"Fucking move it big man," I shouted as I saw torchlight beams at the back of the City Centre Hotel.

"Feel fuckin drunk," said Badge rolling down the window and sticking her face out into the cold air.

"They drugged you I think. Probably in a drink or something," I said.

"Where are we going Coulter and are you paying for the speeding ticket," smiled the big man in the rearview.

"Base big man. Fucking punch it," I replied.

When we reached Base, Badge got out of the car and spewed her ring on the road.

"Oh man," she said in-between retches. "I feel fuckin rotten."

Gerry got out of the car was trying his best to comfort her. It was funny, he looked fucking awkward standing beside her.

"Aye yer awright hen," he said gently patting her back.

Under the glow of the streetlight, I looked at my chest. The tracksuits ultra-high molecular weight polyethylene material had indeed been bullet proof. There were lead pellets stuck within the fibres of my hoodie and I tried to brush them away. Bet I'm going to be bruised as fuck tomorrow. Fucking hell, I thought. My cracked ribs had just about healed. Getting shot by a double-barrelled shotgun wasn't going to help the healing process. If anything, I've probably added to the cracked rib list. The big man helped Badge up the stairs to the house and Jasmine appeared at the front door.

"Oh my God Coulter. What the hell happened," she said looking at my chest.

"It's a long story babe. I'll tell you about it later. Can you help the big man with Badge?"

Jas took over from Gerry and helped Badge into the sitting room Gerry followed me to the kitchen.

"You want a beer or something big man?" I asked.

"I do but better not. Don't want to get the taste for it then I'll not be fit to drive home," he smiled.

"Fuck, I need to get out of these clothes," I said. "Need to check that there's no fucking damage to my body."

"What the fuck happened in there Coulter?" asked Gerry.

"I was lucky to find her big man. There was one guy guarding the room she was in."

"What did you do to him?"

"Let's just say he's retired," I smiled.

"Coulter these Skal Vac cunts are mad. If you've taken out one of their guys they'll be looking for revenge."

"Two," I replied.

"Two what?" asked Gerry.

"I took out two guys. Fucking lucky we went there when we did big man. One of them was trying to rape her. Can you believe it. A fucking fourteen-year-old lassie, man. He won't be doing much raping now. Won't be doing much of anything after I stabbed him right up the jaxy. Left him bleeding out on the floor."

"Fucker got off easy if you ask me. I would've ripped his fucking cock off and stuffed it up his jaxy and let him fuck himself," said the big man with a grin.

"Seriously though, Coulter. These Skal Vac bastards don't like to be fucked with."

"Fuck them Gerry. Fuck the lot of them. They want to take me on – all I can say is fucking bring it."

After the big man departed, Jas took Badge for a bath and changed her into a pair of her pyjamas. The poor lassie was still doped up to the eyeballs but at least she'd stopped spewing. I quickly changed out of my tracksuit and Second-Skin-Suit and was pleasantly surprised to find that aside from some bruising and redness, there was no tissue damage. Fucking result, man! Jas and Badge were sitting on the couch, with Badge curled up and resting her head in Jas's lap. She could barely keep her eyes open, as the adrenaline from the escape had worn off completely.

"So, are you going to tell me what happened tonight or not?" asked Jas.

"It was bad, Jas. Really fucking bad. I arrived just in time to save her," I replied.

When I explained everything that'd transpired, she gave me this look... I cant fucking describe it man. It was a look of love and concern. She knew I took too many risks, but she also knew how I managed to save a young lassie from a truly fucking horrifying experience.

"Coulter," she said, "You take far too many risks. But what you did for her... I love you babe."

"I love you too," I said, kissing her on the cheek. "Can you get her to bed? Let her sleep of the drugs. I need to go next door and send some emails."

"Of course, my darling," she smiled. "Don't be too long, I'll wait up for you."

My Jas, man. My fucking Jas.

First thing I did was to get in touch with Dale and ask if he was interested in publishing a story about the brothel. I couldn't reveal that I helped save Badge, for obvious murder reasons. In his response, he mentioned that brothel stories were not considered newsworthy. Glasgow had plenty of brothels scattered throughout the city. However, if there was any human trafficking involved, then it would definitely grab attention from both him and the police. I had no fucking idea what went on at the City Centre Hotel, but with the Skal Vac mob's reputation, it wouldn't surprise me if they were body smuggling. I planned to ask Badge about it and see what she knew. When I asked for an update on the Toyz4Boyz84 intel, Dale advised me to keep an eye on the newspapers over the next few days. Before going to bed, I shot Dr. Manfred a text informing him that I'd need his mini-MRI services tomorrow.

6.

Badge was up and awake before I was. Jas had gone to work and left her watching some morning TV shit.

"Morning," I said with a smile. "How are you feeling?"

"Got a fuckin brutal headache but Jas gave me some paracetamol. Apart from that am fine."

"Do you know what they gave you?"

"Fuck knows, benzos I think. Cunts forced me tae drink somethin sour."

"What the hell happened. How did you end up in there?"

"They snatched me aff the road. A punter jist picked Sandra up in his motor. Next thing ah know am in the back of a fuckin van. The bastard that punched me the other day wis drivin."

"Fuck sake Badge. I was totally bricking it when Sandra told me. They didn't... You know... Like... Try it on or anything... Before I arrived..."

"Naw did they fuck. They said they wur keepin me fir a VIP who liked young lassies. You came at jist the right time Coulter. That cunt would've did God knows whit tae me. I cannae thank ye enough."

"No bother Badge. I'm just glad you're alright. Listen... You're going have to stay here for a while. Don't want you near the Drag with them cunts about."

"Whit aboot Sandra though, Coulter. She needs ma help. I usually get her hame when she's full of it. She's ma pal. I huv tae look efter her."

Fucking hell man. After all we she's been through, she's still worried about her pal. Have to admit... It was fucking touching.

"Well you're not leaving not until I think it's safe. Don't worry about Sandra. I'll jump the Subway and give her enough money to stay of the Drag for a few days. Just until I work out what to do with these bastards at the City Centre Hotel."

"Before ye dae anythin you'd better fuckin tell me what this is aw aboot. Some cunt blasted ye wi a sawn aff shotgun man and look at ye. It's like fuck aw happened. Ye huv tae fuckin tell me Coulter or am bolting. Thanks fir yer help and aw that."

What could I do? Badge was smart. I couldn't lie to her, so I told her everything. Man. She took in her stride. Didn't even blink a fucking eye when I told her what I did to Cammy Ballater and his crew. Smart and fucking tough. That's Badge alright. One of six. The number of folk who know about Numb seems to be increasing fucking rapidly.

When Dr Manfred showed up, I asked him to give Badge the once over. Told him that somebody had slipped her a mickey. As he was doing her vitals my phone went. It was big Gerry.

"Coulter have you checked the Daily Record online?" he asked.

"I haven't," I said. "I'm a Guardian reader."

"Guardian ma arse. Fucking check it out ASAP and get back to me."

After Badge got the all clear, Dr. Manfred and I we went through to the Med-Bay to do a swift mMRI. He didn't say much about the bruising on my chest until he saw the scan results.

"It looks as if you've added to the number of fractured ribs Coulter, my boy. You really have to look after yourself better," he said.

"It's this new thing I'm trying out with the Jiu-Jitsu. Like new moves and that. It's called Tricking," I lied.

"Whatever it is you're doing you're going to have to take a break... Excuse the pun," he smiled.

"Doc you know I cant. I just can't... You don't know what's going on out there in the streets. Fuck I don't even know. That wee lassie next door knows more than the both of us. People need my help Doc. That's the bottom line."

"Be that as it may. I'm just saying be careful son."

"Aw Doc... I didn't know you cared so much," I said getting up and pulling my t-shit back on.

"There is one thing that might help you recover more speedily," he said.

"And what's that?" I asked.

"Hyperbaric oxygen therapy."

"What the fuck's that when it's at home?

"That's exactly where we will deliver the therapy... At home.

He went on to explain that he'd been in touch with a company who supplied home HBOT. Their top-of-the-line model the OxyNova 10 was available at cost for his clinic and he'd ordered two. One he'd set up in the Med-Bay. I won't tell you how much it cost but let's just say it isn't fucking cheap. The benefits though would be many. Once in the chamber it would deliver 100% of oxygen under pressure to my body – this would speed up the healing process, help stave of infections and generally make me fit as fuck. Not that I wasn't fit. I was. You cant do Jiu fucking Jitsu if you're an unfit slob.

After walking Dr. Manfred to Great Western Road, I headed over to Myra's café to pick up bacon rolls for me and Badge. In the kitchen, the nausea from last night had passed and she was now fucking ravenous. As I munched on my roll smothered in brown sauce, I pulled up the Daily Record website on my phone. The headlines caught my attention – Son of Notorious Gangster Stabbed to Death in City Centre. I realised it wasn't the City Centre Hotel, but rather on Argyle Street. The victim, Michael 'Mad Mickey' Ballater, was dead upon arrival at the Royal Infirmary's A&E. He was the oldest son of Frankie Ballater... Could this be the same cunt that tried to rape Badge? I immediately emailed Dale, whose name was on the article, and asked where exactly Mad Mickey was stabbed, not the fucking location, but his actual body. Within five minutes, Dale responded with a confirmation that he'd been knifed up the shitter. What a fucking bonus man!

"Badge. The guy from last night... he was Frankie Ballater's son," I said with a smirk.

Frankie Ballater? As in the Ballater Boys?" Badge asked, wide-eyed.

The death of that rapist cunt was no loss to the city and would surely make the remaining Ballater Boys fucking nervous. First Cammy, now Mickey... No doubt Frankie would be out for blood and desperate to find out who offed his scumbag son. But fuck him and fuck all of them. One less Ballater in Glasgow was a good thing, and I can guarantee you no one will be mourning his death. It did make me wonder though... Were the Ballaters working with those Skal Vac bastards, or was it just a lucky coincidence? Personally, I didn't believe in coincidences when it came to the bad guys of Glasgow. I fired off an email to Dale Martin and arranged a meet with him later tonight in Partick. It was time to reveal my ID and see if this journo could be fucking trusted.

I asked Jas to take Badge into Partick and get her some clothes and essentials. I warned them both to be cautious and made sure Badge understood the importance of staying away from the Drag. The Skal Vac mob would definitely be on the lookout for her and if they really were connected to the Ballater's, those cunts would be anxious to find her for questioning or worse. I told her that she'd be staying with us for the foreseeable future and there'd be no fucking arguing about it.

When they left, I called the big man.

"I saw the Daily Record headlines. My journo contact confirmed it *was* Mad Mickey, I fucked up in the brothel."

"Good fucking riddance to bad rubbish," said Gerry. "The sooner the city's rid of these Ballater bastards the better."

We talked for a while longer and I shared my concerns about someone possibly recognizing his car. No doubt the Skal Vac mob would be scanning their CCTV footage. But Gerry reassured me, saying he was an Uber driver and drove around that area regularly. If any wannabe gangster cunt confronted him, he'd simply say he was picking up passengers.

I contacted Shenzhen Fabrications – if I was going to take on both the Ballater Boys and the Skal Vac bastards, I was going to need more fucking weapons. I asked if they had anything special they could supply me with. While waiting for their response, I gave Khaled a call at his shop. He had been working on a Kloaker belt that would work together with my Kloaker necklace and make me all but invisible to CCTV cameras. He said it should be ready for testing tomorrow. I also needed new phones for Jas and Badge – something secure with a tracker so I could monitor their movements. Not because I don't trust Jas or anything, but just to be extra fucking cautious. I was more concerned about Badge leaving the house and going to see Sandra in her flat, despite my warnings not to. It reminded me that I needed to go down to the Drag and give some cash to Sandra so she could stay off the streets for a while, at least until things calmed down with the Skal Vac cunts.

Exiting the Subway, I made my way to the Drag. Jas and Badge had decided to have a girls' night in, doing typical girly things. It was funny because I always saw Badge as tomboy; street smart, knew how to handle herself and that, but beneath it all she was still just a fourteen-year-old girl. The only difference between her and other girls her age was that she was born into poverty and addiction. She had to grow up quickly, and I admired her for it. When they returned from shopping they seemed like besties, her and Jas. It was pretty fucking nice to see. As I walked past Central Station, I noticed more and more girls appearing on the streets but none of them were Sandra. I had plans to meet up with Dale in the Quarter Gill on Dumbarton Road at eight, though I did say I might be running a bit late. Taking a detour down Oswald Street, I walked towards the Broomielaw to see if I could find Sandra there. However, as I approached King George V Bridge, I heard a commotion and saw that one lane was blocked off by police cars and crowd had gathered on the riverbank. Curiosity getting the better of me, I made my way through the people towards the river. Kind of fucking wish I hadn't though. Two police boats were hovering underneath the bridge, and upon closer inspection, I saw that they were looking up at something hanging from a metal chain – a naked female body with deep cuts spelling out SK on her back and abdomen. It took me a few seconds to realise that this horrific meat puppet, with its bruised and bloated face was fucking Sandra – Badge's pal. And it was clear that the Skal Vac were responsible for this atrocious display of revenge against Badge's escape. They knew Badge hung around with Sandra, and wanted to send a message to me which was loud and fucking clear. Cruel bastards.

As I rode the train to Partick, my mind was consumed with two thoughts. First, I'd have to tell Badge about Sandra – a conversation I was definitely not looking forward to. And second, how could I get back at those Skal Vac cunts? They were all getting offed that's for fucking sure. When I arrived at the Quarter Gill, Dale was already there. He told me to look for the guy wearing a linen suit, fedora, and glasses bigger than Jeffrey Dahmer's – his words, not mine. I'd told him to watch out for the guy in a green and yellow hoodie with the letter N on his chest. We introduced ourselves and he ordered us drinks – Talisker for him and a bottle of Sol for me. He looked older than I expected; in his sixties at least with a posh fucking English accent. Turns out he's written for all the major British newspapers and has broken some big stories in his career. The Brinks Mat job. The Green Chain Rapist and the fucking Wests house of horrors to name a few. So why the fuck is he writing for the Evening Times and Daily Record? Because he loves Glasgow he said. He doesn't need the work, but he still has a hunger to seek out stories that no one else will touch. Gotta admire the guy for that. Fucking respect is due. We began discussing the Toyz4Boyz84 story, and he told me he had an agreement with his contact at Police Scotland to run it on the day of the planned police raids at multiple locations. According to his contact, it could happen any day now. I couldn't fucking wait to see those sick pedo cunts behind bars in the Bar L. My fervent fucking hope was that the other prisoners would make their lives a fucking misery. No cunt in prison likes a nonce.

"Coulter, I have to ask you... Why?"

"Why what?"

"Why are you doing what you're doing. Most people are happy to work their nine to five and spend their evenings watching Strictly Come Dancing or Bake Off."

"Do you remember the story a while back about the drunk driver crashing over the Kingston Bridge into the Clyde?" I asked.

"Yes, I do," Dale replied.

"That was my parents. I can tell you this... My dad never got behind the wheel if he'd been drinking. He rarely drank."

"Really?"

"Aye, really. It was the Ballater Boys. Cammy Ballater and his crew to be specific. They ran him off the road and into the river."

"How come I have never heard this?" asked Dale incredulously.

"Fucking Ballater money covered it up, and I found out about it. You know what happened to Cammy Ballater?" I asked.

"I read he was taken out by a rival gang," said Dale.

"That was no gang... It was me. I fucking offed him and his crew, and his brothers are on my fucking Wishlist. Mad Mickey was a unexpected bonus for me – I didn't even know who the cunt was."

"Michael Ballater? That was you? So that's why you were so interested in the location of his unfortunate terminal injury," he smiled.

"You're right," I winked.

"Listen Coulter, I found the story about your parents hard to believe. Someone accidently driving off the Kingston Bridge? Really? I met them you know," said Dale.

"My folks? When?"

"Oh... It was few years back. A charity do I believe. Your mum was the keynote speaker. I remember your dad joking to me that he was just a glorified chauffer."

"Aye... That was dad alright," I said. A huge pang of... Something in my chest.

"So... To answer your question Dale... I'm doing it for my mum and dad, but I'm also doing it for the city. For the weak, the defenceless, for those that cant fight back. You know the charity work mum was involved in... Well this is just a continuation of her work," I smiled. "My mission is to rid the city of cunts like Skal Vac and the Ballater bawbags."

Next, I told him about Numb and how I wanted to help the good people of Glasgow. He seemed a bit puzzled at first, but once he saw that I was fucking determined and capable of carrying out my plans, he nodded in understanding. I also made sure to mention that money wasn't an issue for me as I was totally fucking minted, which is definitely an advantage in the world of crime fighting. Of course, it went without saying that nobody can know about my alter ego and my future missions. Dale simply winked at me and finished his drink with a knowing smile. And with that he became one of seven.

At the bar I ordered another bottle of Sol and bought Dale a double malt.

"What do know about the Skal Vac mob Dale?"

"They're serious. That I know. They have an active cell here in the city. Running women and drugs."

"You know that I didn't off Mad Mickey on Argyle Street. The cunt was in the City Centre Hotel... Have you heard of it?"

"Who hasn't. That's where Skal Vac run their operation. Why were you there?"

"Listen I didn't know who the cunt was. All I know was that a friend of mine was snatched by the Skal Vac and the Ballater bastard was just about to rape her. I got there just in fucking time Dale. It was her pal Sandra who told me where to find her – Sandra who was found earlier hanging naked from the King George V bridge with SV carved on her front and back." I said.

"I heard about it on the police scanner. So you think they murdered her because you killed Mad Mickey and saved your friend?" asked Dale.

"That's exactly what I'm saying, and I need your help to get the cunts who killed her. It's nit fucking right, Dale. What? Just because she told me where her pal was she had to die? Just because she's an addict and has to sell herself to feed her habit – those bastards think they can get away with killing her because they think she's scum. That she meant nothing... Fuck that. She was somebody's daughter. Somebody's sister. She was somebody Dale."

"Going after them won't be easy. The only thing going for you is that they're a small unit. I believe there's a core of six," said Dale.

"Eh... Five... One of them blew his head of... Or least what remained of his head, with a shotgun," I smiled.

"Ok... Five. My advice is to hit them at the City Centre and do it quick. Don't wait until more of them come over from the old country. Early Sunday morning I'd say. Most, if not all of the punter's will be gone. I heard they minibus the girls to house in Drumchapel when they are done for the night."

"How do you know all this?" I asked.

"I'm a reporter. I've got informants on both sides of the law, and I've been looking for a Skal Vac story that was more than just about brothels in Glasgow. If you're going to take them out then that's a story I'd be interested in... First hand."

"What? You want to come with me?" I smiled.

"Maybe not exactly with you... But nearby. Just give me a tip-off... I'll do the rest."

After one more drink, Dale called an Uber, and I jumped the last train back to Kelvinbridge, I saved his mobile number on my Pixel and asked him to check his WhatsApp over the weekend.

7.

Badge man. Fuck… She was so upset when I told her about Sandra. Poor lassie ended up spewing her ring in the bog. It hit her hard, man. Sandra was like a sister or even a mother figure to her. The fact that she was an addict and a prostitute didn't fucking matter. Man, I think after mum and dad, that's the worse I've ever felt… Seeing that wee lassie in such despair. Heart-breaking. Fucking Skal Vac cunts. But at least Jas was there for her, comforting her while I came up with a plan to kick some eastern European arse… And by kick some arse, I mean kill the fucking lot of them.

I stopped by Khaled's shop on Friday afternoon to pick up the Kloaker belt. My Sunday early morning plan required it. He was in the shop on his tod serving a customer. He motioned for me to wait in the back workshop. Once finished with the customer he came back and his usual cheerful demeanour was nowhere to be seen.

"What's wrong with your pus?" I asked.

"It's Saleem, man. He got jumped yesterday on the way back from college," he replied.

Saleem was doing a part-time course in electronics and computer maintenance at Stow College.

"What the fuck man?" I said. "Is he alright?"

"Cunt's gave him a right doin Coulter, but he's alright. Bruised to fuck but no bones broken. Had to take him to the Royal's A&E… Waited eight fucking hours man. All his x-rays and that were normal."

"Thank fuck for that. Does he know who did it?"

"He said there's been a group of rocket's noising students up lately but they never bothered him. You know Saleem man. He wouldn't say boo to a fucking goose."

Khaled was right. Saleem was a quiet guy. When I first met him it took ages to get a fucking conversation going he was that shy.

"When they were battering him they were shouting 'Fuckin Packie bastard. Go back tae yer ain country' bunch of cunts."

Khaled's folks were originally from Kerala in India. Khaled and Saleem were as Scottish as me or you.

"When is he going back to Stow?" I asked.

"He's scared Coulter man. Probably he'll take a week off and then he'll need to go to class."

"No problem. Let me know and I'll go meet him after. I'll make sure nobody fucks with him."

"Brilliant. I'll let him know. He'll be chuffed. Cheers bro."

"What can I say... I'm just a nice guy," I grinned.

"Aye right!" smiled Khaled.

"So... What about this belt?" I asked.

"Got it right here my man. It's a fucking beauty. Even made it elasticated in case you get fat ya dobber."

In his hand was a yellow, red and black striped belt with s snake shaped buckle.

"A fucking snake-belt Khaled? What... Are we going back to the seventies," I said.

"Made it myself. Bought a snake-belt from eBay and then 3D scanned it. I've got a pal who has a 3D metal printer. Had to make it a bit bigger than the original. You know... For the electrics and that. Try it on," he said with a big fucking grin.

I clipped it round my waste. The thing was tight but not uncomfortable.

"Outside you go," said Khaled.

I knew the drill – stand outside the shop door and look up at the security camera. I was already wearing the Kloaker necklace and now with the belt, I should be fucking invisible.

Back in the workshop I asked Khaled how it looked. He'd taken a screenshot and all you could see were my trainers. Above them was a wobbling distortion that most cunts would blame on the camera.

"Might need to work on it to boost the power more so that your feet are not showing," said Khaled.

"Listen, I need it now. It'll be fine. I'll be using it in the dark so don't worry about my fucking trainers."

"Worry about you? Never," Khaled smiled.

I promised Khaled I'd return the belt at the start of the week. A few minutes after leaving the shop, Dale sent me a WhatsApp. His source had tipped him off about the City Centre Hotel's basement strong room where the Skal Vac mob would be counting their money and sorting their drugs on Sunday morning. Walking back to Base, I had Caroline Polachek's latest album blasting through my XM5's – you really need to check it out, man. It's fucking tops.

Badge seemed to be doing better after Jas managed to feed her some dinner. When I told her my plan to take revenge on Sandra's killers, she insisted on coming with me. I fucking refused, knowing how dangerous the Skal Vac mob was. But Badge wouldn't give up easily. Eventually she understood I had to do it on my own. In preparation for Sunday, I did some research on the buildings in Richard Street and found out that the City Centre the offices of a tobacco baron – that's why there was a strong room in the basement. Those robbing cunts made loads of money during the days of slavery and a strong room was probably far safer than housing their riches in a bank. I manged to find an old blueprint of the building. The size of the basement was surprisingly large, and the door was made of metal. It was like the world's largest fucking safe but it ignited an idea on how I was going to make the Skal Vac suffer for what they did to Badge and Sandra. I phoned the big man and asked him if he was up for an early Sunday morning adventure. He was.

8.

At three in the morning, Big Gerry arrived to pick me up. I had my backpack with all my weapons of revenge, but I asked him to stop at a filling station so I could grab two gallons of petrol.

"You do realise this is an electric car Coulter?" laughed the big man.

"Ha fucking ha," I replied.

We parked on the corner of Richard Street – there was a fair bit of activity at the City Centre Hotel. At five o'clock, a Transit mini-bus pulled up and several girls got inside. Once it drove off, I prepared my gear. This would be the first time using my full face-mask with night vision and augmented reality. When I put it on, Big Gerry couldn't help but laugh.

"It's a fucking improvement," he said sarcastically.

"Arsehole," I muttered back.

A message from Dale informed me he was waiting at the other end of the street. The plan I had in store would definitely make the fucking headlines. With my blade on my waist and the Eraser Taser in my hand, I stepped out of the motor and grabbed the container of petrol from the boot. Time was of the essence as I made my way to the back of the building, where Badge and I had escaped before. Climbing through the hole in the fence was fucking easier than scaling two brick walls. Kloaker was activated and my in-mask display provided crucial GPS information. The red dot indicating Gerry's car flashed on-screen – a reassuring sight. My mask may have been lightweight, but it was completely fucking bullet-proof, even though I had no intention of getting shot in the face today, or any other fucking day for that matter. As luck would have it, the ground floor door at the back of the brothel was electronically locked and opened easily with my sov ring. Now came the tricky part – sneaking through the dark corridor. According to the old blueprints I found online, the stairwell leading to the basement was in the middle of the hall. I heard muffled voices and readied the ET for a kill shot. At the top of the stairs, I saw a slither of light coming from beneath the strong room door in the basement. For my plan to fucking work, that door had to be made of metal. Just as I was about to make my way down, the fucking door opened and guy was talking loudly on his mobile phone. I quickly hid behind the wall. Hoping he'd just opened the door for better reception. No fucking luck though. Someone yelled something to him in a foreign language and he closed the strong room door, making his way up the stairs. I placed the ET and petrol can on the floor, preparing for an attack. When he reached the top, he stopped to light a fag. Thankfully, he didn't fucking bother turning on any lights as he walked towards the front door because if he had, he would have seen me sneaking up behind him and it would have ruined the fucking surprise. I waited to see if he'd finish his call, but it seemed he wasn't going to anytime soon. Fuck it. I sprang into action and caught him in a rear chokehold, using my Jiu Jitsu strength. He dropped his phone and the fag as he tried to extricate himself from my grip – the chokehold rendered him unable to make a fucking sound. He was losing consciousness fast, but I didn't want him knocked out yet. I pulled the hunting knife from my waistband and raised it high above his napper before plunging it deep into his skull with one swift motion. A perfect fucking kill. He stopped struggling and made gurgling noises as I propped him up against the wall. Time was fucking ticking. I grabbed the ET and the petrol can and headed back down the stairs. The door was the original; pure metal at it's finest. I heard laughter coming from inside and couldn't help but smile behind my mask. That laughter would soon turn to screams of terror. With the Eraser Taser set to its highest level of close contact tasing, I placed it right next to the door lock and pulled the trigger. The intense heat coming from this baby melted the metal and sealed the door shut. Best part was, it was almost completely silent. Inside, the laughter continued, so I stood still for a moment, allowing for the metal to solidify. Grabbing the petrol can, I began pouring petrol on the floor, making sure that it ran through the crack at the bottom of the door. I doubted anyone would notice until the could smell it. As I walked back up the stairs, I left a large trail of accelerant behind me. When I reached the dead cunt in the hallway, I fired a Limpet Bullet from the ET to set the petrol alight. The fire spread quickly down the stairs and through the strong room door. I didn't hear an alarm or see any sprinklers going off. My plan was to burn the whole building down to the fucking ground. The basement would become an inferno, and those cunts inside wouldn't stand a fucking chance. The flames were already climbing up the walls and across the ceiling, engulfing everything in their path. I grabbed the dead guy with the knife in his dome and dragged him outside. The heat was intense, but it was beautiful, man. Closing the front door I propped the cunt up in a ghastly fucking pose before pulling out my Pixel and calling Dale.

"If you want a good photo, I'd come now," I said and took off towards the big man's car.

Getting into the front seat, I saw Dales car pull round and with his phone he took a few snaps of the dead Skal Vac with the knife buried deep in his head. We waited and watched the fire climb to the second and third floor. By then we heard sirens in the distance. The Fire Brigade were on their way. Dale would hang about but not us – we were fucking offski. Back to the West End as the early morning sky turned from dark to light. Jas and Badge were curled up on the couch when I got back. Sleeping like beautiful babies. I crept up the stair to have a quick shower and dump my stuff at Base. When I came back down to the lounge Badge woke up.

"Whit time is it?" she asked sleepily.

"It's early. Go back to sleep," I whispered.

Jas turned her head but didn't wake up.

"Is it done Coulter. Did ye get them back fir whit they did tae Sandra?"

"Aye," I said. "It's done."

"Good," she replied with a smile, pulling the cover up and going back to sleep.

The Monday headlines in all the newspapers, whether tabloid or broadsheet, were sensational. Dale had shared the photo of the deceased

Skal Vac cunt and it was picked up by all the papers. Everything was working out fucking wonderfully. In the afternoon, he called me with two more pieces of good news. Firstly, the pedo raids had taken place and the Evening Times had the exclusive story. There was definitely a lot of unhappy fucking pedos across the city today. Secondly, he told me he'd waited at the City Centre Hotel until the blaze was completely extinguished and had talked to a firefighter who broke through the basement. The gory details of unrecognizable bodies melted together was fucking music to my ears. That old song played in my head. You know the one, but I changed the lyrics to 'I do like Mondays.'

About the Author

Raymond Moore is the author of several books including Sex & Drugs & Rock & Roll and Nursing, The Mournful One, The Daedalus (as G.I. Noah), Castledawn and the Skye Stories Trilogy and Numb Volume 1. Raymond was born in Glasgow. Schooled on the Isle of Skye. Educated in Edinburgh. Works in Saudi Arabia. Loves Thailand.